Teresa Lynch & Korky Paul

Call Me Sam

Oxford University Press
Oxford New York Toronto

My name is Samuel David.
Mostly I'm called Sam.
But just between the two of us
I wonder who I am.

Whenever I am climbing,
Or swinging on my bed,
Daddy calls me monkey
And pats me on the head.

I don't think I'm a monkey,
I don't live up a tree,
Though I like a sliced banana
On ice-cream for my tea.

It’s true I keep on talking,
I’ve got a lot to say,
People call me parrot,
In a laughing sort of way.

I don't think I'm a parrot,
Though my eyes and clothes are bright.
I tried flapping from a gum tree,
And gave myself a fright.

And then they call me Big Ears
(That's mostly Mum and Dad).
'Here's our own dear little rabbit.'
Well, it makes me hopping mad.

I don't think I'm a rabbit.
I don't have a twitching nose.
My ears are only little,
But they hear a lot, I suppose.

When they're in a hurry,
People say, 'You're very slow.
Come on, little tortoise.
It's nearly time to go.'

I don't think I'm a tortoise,
Though I wouldn't mind a shell,
Then I could hide myself away,
But I couldn't climb so well.

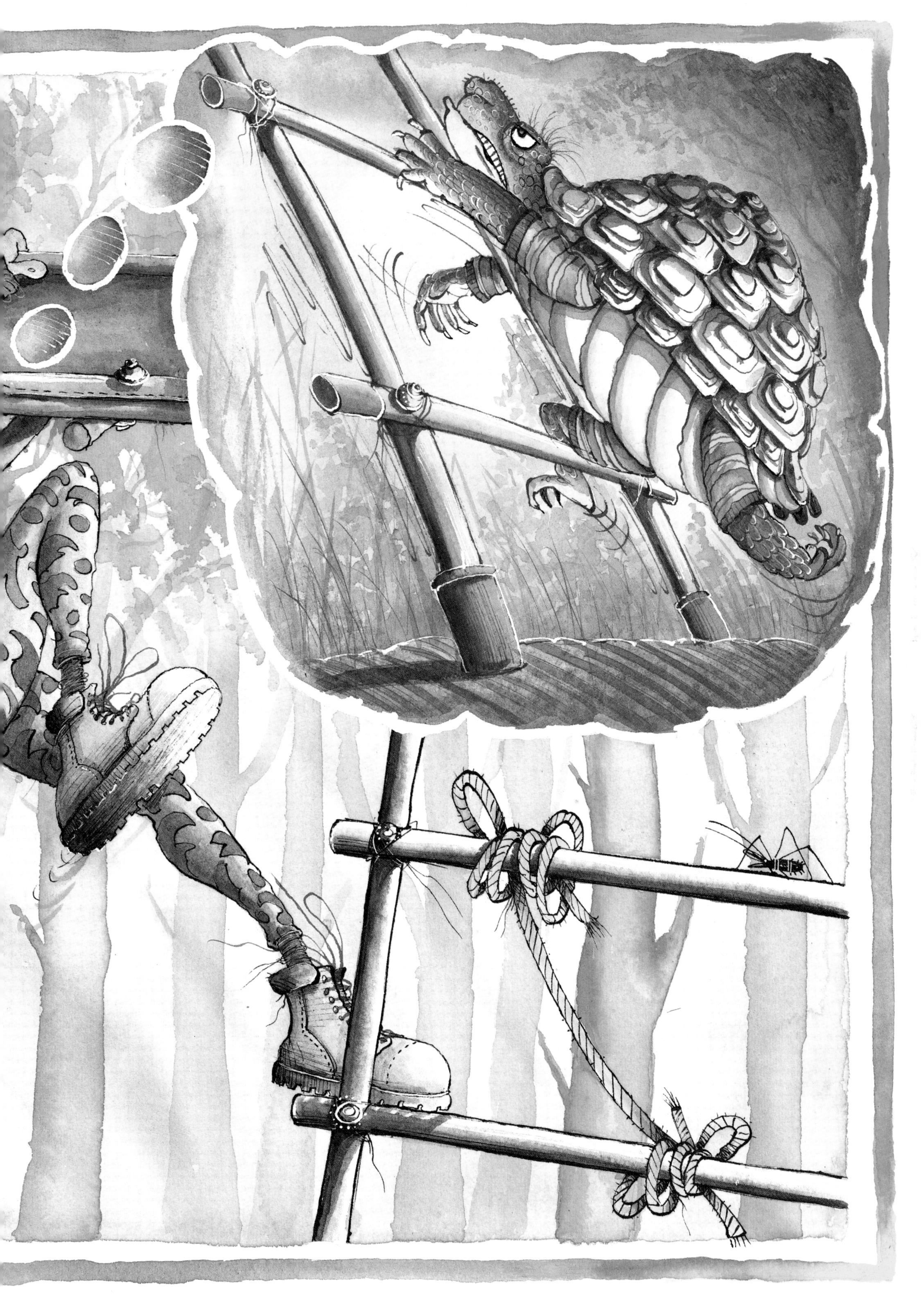

When I stamp my brand new boots
Down on the kitchen floor,
They nickname me the elephant
And shoo me out the door.

I don't think I'm an elephant
Though I love to stomp around.
My nose is short and stumpy,
I can't make a trumpet sound.

Right up on Daddy's shoulders,
I perch myself so high.
He calls me wriggly-jiggly-worm,
I always wonder why.

I don't think I'm a worm,
Because I love the shining sun.
Though I often spend time digging
Holes and tunnels just for fun.

I've asked a thousand times
For them to tell me who I am.
My name is Samuel David,
But please . . . just call me SAM!